W9-CCO-163

Tiptoe Tapirs

HANMIN KIM

Holiday House / New York

This story took place long ago in
a jungle where many animals lived.
The jungle looks peaceful, doesn't it?

In fact, the jungle was a very noisy place. The elephant went BOOM-BOOM! The rhinoceros went BAM-BAM! The hornbill went CAW-CAW! And the ape went HOO-HAA-HOO-HAA! Each animal tried to be louder than the others . . .

except for Tapir, who tiptoed about the jungle ever so softly. How silent and gentle she was. She was so silent that when she went for a walk with Little Tapir, no one knew they were passing by.

Tapir and Little Tapir did not wish to disturb anything or anyone.

Tiptoe, tiptoe.
They were careful not
to step on a flower.

Tiptoe, tiptoe.
They were careful not
to step on an ant.

Hush, hush, hush.
They were careful not to disturb
the resting crocodiles.

Tapir and Little Tapir lived in a cozy home under a tree. It was the quietest place in the jungle.

On the morning of her third birthday, Little Tapir wished to go to the Great Puddle to eat mud cakes.

So Tapir and Little Tapir set out to take a long,
silent walk past the waterfall and along the stream.

They were so quiet that no one knew they
were passing by.

When they arrived at the Great Puddle, a porcupine couple was already there. But no matter. There was plenty of mud for everyone. And it was delicious. Then, out of the blue . . .

THUD, THUD, THUD . . .

GROWL!

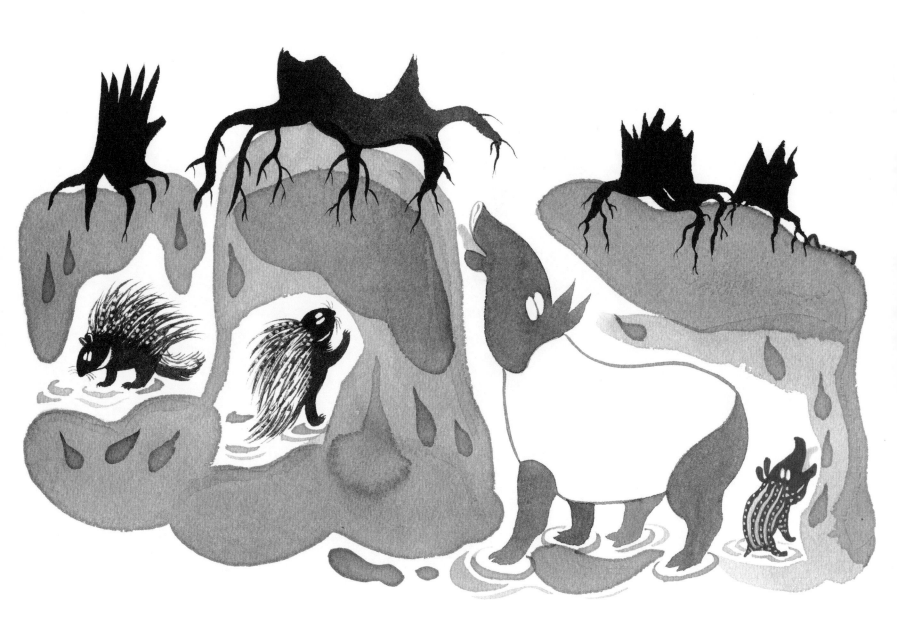

A leopard attacked.
The tapirs ran.

The leopard ran with loud, heavy steps.
THUD, THUD, THUD.

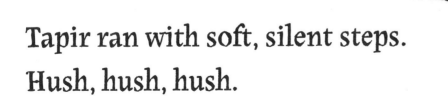

Tapir ran with soft, silent steps.
Hush, hush, hush.

But the leopard was faster!
He was just about to sink his teeth
into Tapir when . . .

BANG! BANG! BANG!

It was the hunter's shotgun.

The leopard was terrified. He crouched on his hind legs and hid his eyes with his paw. He was so paralyzed with fear that he couldn't run away. Seeing this, the kindhearted Little Tapir whispered, "We can help you, Mr. Leopard."

Tapir tiptoed softly. Hush, hush. Little Tapir tiptoed softly. Hush, hush. And the leopard tiptoed softly too. Hush, hush.

Tapir, Little Tapir and the leopard escaped!
And from that day on, the leopard learned
to move with a very soft step.

And as talk spreads quickly in the jungle, the animals no longer tried to be the loudest. Now each tried to be the quietest of all.

And the hunter, who thought all the animals were gone, left the jungle, never to return.

Library of Congress Cataloging-in-Publication Data

Kim, Han-min, 1979 – author, illustrator.

[Sappun sappun ttappiru. English]

Tiptoe tapirs / Hanmin Kim ; English translation by Sera Lee. — First American edition.

pages cm

"First published in Korea as TAPIR'S SOFT STEPS in 2013 by BIR Publishing Co., Ltd., Seoul."

Summary: Tapir and Little Tapir are the quietest creatures in a very noisy jungle, but when a leopard is threatened by a hunter they teach him how to move with a very soft step, and the other animals follow suit.

ISBN 978-0-8234-3395-7 (hardcover)

[1. Tapirs—Fiction. 2. Jungle animals—Fiction. 3. Noise—Fiction.

4. Jungles—Fiction.] I. Lee, Sera, translator. II. Title.

PZ7.1.K56Tip 2015

[E]—dc23

2014032300